MONSTER BUDDIES

I'LL HAUNT YOU!

MEET A GHOST

Shannon Knudsen

illustrated by Chiara Buccheri

M MILLBROOK PRESS ★ MINNEAPOLIS

For Kay Knudsen, an inspiration —S.K

This is for Ale —C.B.

Text and illustrations copyright © 2015 by Lerner Publishing Group, Inc.

All rights reserved. International copyright secured. No part of this book may be reproduced, stored in a retrieval system, or transmitted in any form or by any means—electronic, mechanical, photocopying, recording, or otherwise—without the prior written permission of Lerner Publishing Group, Inc., except for the inclusion of brief quotations in an acknowledged review.

Millbrook Press
A division of Lerner Publishing Group, Inc.
241 First Avenue North
Minneapolis, MN 55401 USA

For reading levels and more information, look up this title at www.lernerbooks.com.

Main body text set in Sunshine Regular 17/24.
Typeface provided by Chank.

Library of Congress Cataloging-in-Publication Data

Knudsen, Shannon, 1971–
    I'll haunt you!: Meet a ghost / by Shannon Knudsen ; illustrated by Chiara Buccheri.
        pages   cm. — (Monster Buddies)
    ISBN 978-0-7613-9186-9 (lib. bdg. : alk. paper)
    ISBN 978-1-4677-4776-9 (eBook)
    1. Ghosts—Juvenile literature. I. Buccheri, Chiara - ill. II. Title.
BF1461.K58 2015
133.1—dc23   2013033473

Manufactured in the United States of America
1 – BOL – 7/15/14

TABLE OF CONTENTS

Meet a Ghost

Woooooooooo . . . Woooooooooo . . .
Are you scared yet? You should be! That's
my creepiest moan. My name's Pablo.

I'm a ghost.

A ghost is the spirit of a dead person. Think of me as the part that stayed behind when my body died.

Your Guide to Ghosts

Have you ever seen a ghost? Not a chance!
Ghosts aren't real. I won't be floating into
your room at night.

You'll find plenty of us in scary stories, though. Some ghosts look like they're made of fog. Some look like people, except you can see right through them. And some ghosts are invisible.

You can't see them at all.

Ghosts like to haunt places that are special to them. We often stick around the spot where we lived—or died. We can also haunt people by following them around. We play lots of tricks too.

My favorite place to haunt is my old house.
I make the lights flash on and off. That really
spooks the folks who just moved in!

Not all ghosts want to scare people. Some of us just want to say hello to our loved ones. Sometimes we have a message to give them. My buddy Morgan haunts a parking lot.

He warns people to drive safely!

One of my favorite tricks is sneaking up on people. Since I don't have a body, I can whoosh through walls and slide through doors. Don't bother trying to lock me out!

Of course, not having a body can be hard. My fingers swish through everything I touch. And I miss eating. I would trade moving through walls for one piece of pizza.

Suppose you have a ghost problem.

What should you do?

BLUE

Some folks think blue paint will keep ghosts away. That's because the blue looks like water, and some ghosts can't cross water. Other people spread beans or seeds on the floor. A ghost might stop to count every single seed. That takes a while!

You might try just asking the ghost not to bother you. But be polite!

Ghosts Near and Far

No matter where you go in the world, you'll hear ghost stories. The Weeping Woman is a famous ghost from Mexico. She wanders the land at night, crying. Some say she's searching for her lost children.

Watch out for her claws!

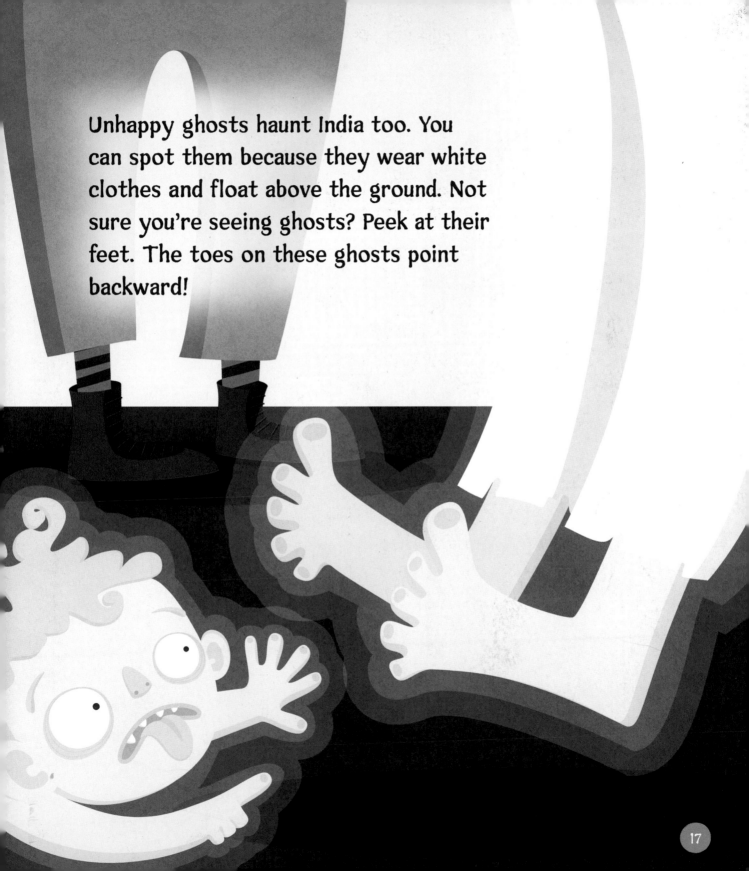

Unhappy ghosts haunt India too. You can spot them because they wear white clothes and float above the ground. Not sure you're seeing ghosts? Peek at their feet. The toes on these ghosts point backward!

In China, living people honor their ancestors by putting food out for them. What about the dead people who have no relatives to honor them? They return as ghosts each fall.

Of course, no one wants a lonely ghost hanging around. To help their visitors feel better, the Chinese celebrate the Hungry Ghost Festival. They offer food to the ghosts. They also put paper boats in the water. The floating boats show the ghosts the way home.

That's the spooky truth about ghosts. But don't worry. I promise not to play any tricks on you. Really! Cross my heart and hope to...

BOOOO!

A Ghost's Day Writing Activity

You've learned a lot about ghosts. Now it's time to scare your friends with some spooky facts. Grab a pencil and a piece of paper. Write a short story about what a ghost's day is like. Does it haunt a house with its friends? Does it make creepy noises? What does it do for fun? Draw a picture to go with your story.

GLOSSARY

ancestors: family members who lived before a person and have died

haunt: to visit a place or a person as a ghost

invisible: not able to be seen

spirit: a part of a person that lives on after the person dies

23

TO LEARN MORE

Books

Hamilton, Martha, and **Mitch Weiss.** *The Ghost Catcher.* Atlanta: August House Little Folk, 2008.
In this Bengali folktale, a barber uses a mirror to scare a ghost into helping him.

Krensky, Stephen. *Ghosts.* Minneapolis: Lerner Publications, 2008.
This nonfiction book gives the scary scoop on ghosts of all kinds.

Paquette, Ammi-Joan. *Ghost in the House.* Somerville, MA: Candlewick Press, 2013.
A clever young witch figures out how to deal with the ghosts who haunt her house in this picture book.

Websites

The Learning Channel: Ghost Stories
http://tlc.howstuffworks.com/family/ghost-stories.htm
Scare your friends with this site's spooky ghost tales, written just for kids.

PBS Kids: Happy Halloween
http://pbskids.org/halloween
In the mood for something spooky? Visit this website for fun, Halloween-themed activities.

INDEX